Nia and the New Free Library

By Ian Lendler   Illustrated by Mark Pett

chronicle books · san francisco

For as long as anyone could remember,
the Littletown Library stood there.

It was there so long . . .

Until one day, a tornado came
and carried the whole thing away.

that people stopped paying attention.
The building got old.
The librarian retired.
And nobody noticed.

No one quite knew what to do with the
empty space where the library used to be.

"We need a biiiig skyscraper," said the builder.
"That will really put this town on the map."

"We need a parking lot," said the grocer.
"That would help my business."

But Nia had a different idea.

"We need to rebuild the library."

"Rebuild it?" said the Mayor.

"What's the point?
No one uses libraries anymore."

"Rebuild it?" said the banker.
"That costs money, and I can't spare a dime."

"Who needs it?"
said a distracted mom.

"My son and I get everything
we want online."

"I'm on level ten!"

But Nia loved the library. She went every week to check out books. She liked cookbooks the best. Her favorite spot to read them was under the tree in front of the library.

But it's hard to check out a book from a library that isn't there.

That's when Nia had an idea.

She got a desk

and a chair.

And a pencil and
some paper.

And a plate of orange
slices for energy.

Then, she began to write.
It took her all day.

It took her another day, too.

From sunup to sundown, it took her a lot of days.

And at first, no one paid any attention.

But pretty soon, she had written an entire wagon full of books.

"Would you like to check out a book?" she asked the grocer.

"How?" he said. "The library is gone."

"This is the *new* Free Library," said Nia.

The grocer was curious, so he picked up the book on top of the pile and began to read:

"There was an old lady who lived in a shoe. She lived in a shoe? *PEE-YEW!*"

"Hey!" said the grocer.
"You wrote this wrong!"

"I did?" said Nia.
"Well, maybe you can fix it."

She handed the grocer a pencil. The grocer started to write.

"Excuse me," said the distracted mom.

"My son's phone just died. Could he look at one of your books?"

"Of course," Nia said. "This is the new Free Library. He can read any book he likes. This one is about Sir Wilbur, the bravest, most handsome knight around."

"This is terrible!" said the boy. "*I* can draw better than that!"

"You're probably right," said Nia. "Maybe you can fix it."

As they made more books, more townspeople became curious and stopped to look.

The town's detective saw the crowd forming and came over to see if there was any trouble. She picked up a book. "This was my favorite book growing up!"

"And this book is the reason I fell in love with the sea," said the boat captain.

But as they read, everybody noticed mistakes.

"Arrr!" said the boat captain.

"*Where The Mild Things Roam*?! That's not the title!"

"And that's not how Sherlock solved the crime!" said the detective.

Every time, Nia simply said, "Oh. Well, maybe you can fix it."

And she handed them a pencil.

Pretty soon, half the town was writing alongside Nia.

"Whaddya think?"

"I've never built a house-shoe before."

"How are the sketches going?"

"I'm on page ten!"

Everyone discovered the job was
a lot harder than it looked.

"You're wrong! That
clue was a red herring."

" . . . and that's
how he solved
the crime!"

"There was a fish
in the story?"

"I'm confused."

But they began to remember words and ideas
that had inspired them.

" . . . like hopes springing high,
Still I'll rise."

"I love poems about bread."

Pretty soon, there were enormous piles of freshly written books. Books of adventure and poetry, and filled with every idea ever imagined.

There were so many books that they spilled into the road and stopped traffic.

"Hmmmm," said Nia. "If only there was some better way to organize them."

"I've got empty crates
we could use as shelves,"
said the grocer.

"If it rains, the books
will get wet," said the builder.

"I'll make some walls and
a roof to protect them."

"And we'll need lions,"
said the banker.

"A good library *has* to have
lions in front. I'll get the
two from my bank."

Pretty soon the entire
town was lending a hand.

There were people writing and drawing and binding and building and sorting and stacking and slicing oranges for energy.

ORANGES

"What we need is an opening ceremony!" said the Mayor.

So the Mayor fetched her shiniest ribbon and her biggest scissors and her fanciest outfit, and she was just about to cut the ribbon so the crowd could shout "Hooray!" when Nia said . . .

"Wait! We forgot one thing."

"We did?"
said the builder.

"We did?"
said the banker.

"We have a library,"
said Nia.

"But we
don't have
a librarian."

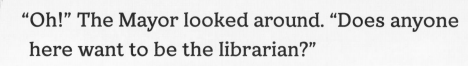 "Oh!" The Mayor looked around. "Does anyone here want to be the librarian?"

"That should fix it," said Nia.

Then the Mayor cut the ribbon.

The whole town shouted **"Hooray!"**

And Littletown's New Free Library was open.

Everyone crowded into the library
to admire what they had accomplished.

"I decided to go for
a classic feel with
watercolors..."

There were kids in beanbags reading picture books. Kids with pencils writing new books.

In one corner, there was a knitting class. In another, all the grandparents were learning to use a computer.

"First, we make sure it's plugged in . . ."

Everywhere there were people sitting together, enjoying the cozy quiet of a book-filled place.

Meanwhile, Nia did what she had wanted to do from the very beginning. She quietly walked straight to her favorite section . . . and checked out her favorite book.

How to Make Stone Soup

by Nia

LIBRA

And she sat down to read in her favorite spot underneath the library's tree.

At least she did . . .

Until the tornado came back and carried the school away.

Sigh.

The End

Author's Note

When I was little, my grandfather told me that he hated the old library in our town.

It was too small, too dark. There wasn't enough room for people to meet. There weren't enough books.

He wanted our town to have a library that was open and full of light. Where kids could have their own section to make noise. Where people could enjoy as many books as they liked.

My grandfather was a lawyer, so he got the town to agree to a plan, he got all the permits, and raised the money to build it.

The day of the Opening Ceremony for the new library, I was the proudest kid in town. There was a big party, and I went around telling everyone that my grandfather had built the library.

Then, I met the son of the Head Librarian. He was walking around telling everyone that his mother had picked all the books on the shelves, the art on the walls, and the chairs and tables. He told everyone that his mother had built the library.

Then, I met the builder's daughter. She told everyone that her dad had built the library. He had poured the cement foundation and laid down all the bricks.

That's when I noticed that every brick on the path that led to the entrance of the building was engraved with the name of a family who had donated time, love, and money to get the job done.

That's when I realized—a library is an expression of a town and all the people who live in it.

A library is built by many hands.